Little Lives Matter

BRAVE BOOKS

N
W
E
S
DOM-A-TRON
Doomsdome
THE OLD ISL
Burrycan
UTOPIA
Freedom Island
WIGGAMORE WOODS
SUMA SAVANNA
Rushington
Hive Haven
Furenzy park
Toke-A-Toke
Wonder Well
Capitol
Mushroom Village
Deserted Desert
RAKA RAIN FOREST
Mt. Avalerif
Sky Tree
Snapfast Meadow
CAR-A-LAGO COAST
Starlotte City
Gray Landing

Home of the Brave

Welcome to **Freedom Island**, Home of the Brave, where good battles evil and truth prevails. Years ago, the legends of Freedom Island fought to create a free nation. Now, as evil forces press closer, a new generation must arise to defend it.

Watch this video for an introduction to the story and BRAVE universe!

Saga One: The Origins
Book 2

Little Lives Matter

Shivermore

Nogard Cavern

MONOCK MOUNTAINS

Meltonville

CABAL ISLAND

Temple of The Serpent

Saga One: The Origins—Book 2

Little Lives Matter

Copyright © 2021 by BRAVE BOOKS.
All Rights Reserved.

Book Illustrations © 2021 by Sergio R. Romeri
Map Illustration © 2021 by Ali Elzeiny

Published by BRAVE BOOKS
www.BRAVEbooks.us

ISBN: 978-1-955550-01-7 (paperback)

First edition published in the USA in 2021 by BRAVE BOOKS

Printed in Canada.

Little Lives Matter

BRAVE BOOKS and **Elizabeth Johnston**

Art by **Sergio R. Romeri**

BRAVE
BOOKS

Just as the wildflowers were starting to bloom in Wiggamore Woods, the sweetest little bear cub was born. He wasn't like any other cub on Freedom Island, but that made Mother Bear love him even more.

Little Mobi had two brown bear eyes, one brown bear nose, two brown bear feet, and ten little toes. But Little Mobi had only one front paw, so Mother Bear cared for her frail little cub day and night.

One evening, Mother Bear was rocking Little Mobi when Culture the Vulture landed beside her. "What a tired mother you are," he squawked. "How hard you work caring for such a small, weak baby."

"When you're stuck with him, you can't climb trees with friends. Why don't you leave him and live for yourself?"

"Zip it, Culture!" growled Mother Bear.

"Go away; let us be! My life may be hard, but my son's still my son, and I love him even more than all the treetops filled with fun. You say if I leave, then my life will be free, but it's my son's life, not mine, that means most to me."

Just as Culture promised, the years got tough, but Little
Mobi got tougher. And bit by bit, he grew.

Soon Little Mobi learned to play with other bear cubs. He fished with them and wrestled with them and tracked mud through his mother's den with them. But his friends' favorite thing was climbing the big oak tree in the center of the forest.

As they climbed to the tippity-top, Little Mobi watched from below, wishing he wasn't missing a paw.

One day, a friend called down, "Come on, Mobi, won't you try climbing too?"

Little Mobi looked down at his one little paw and up to the tippity-top of the tree.

With a shake of his ears and a huff and a grunt, Mobi decided to climb.

One arm up, two legs up. One arm higher, two legs higher. Inch by inch Little Mobi climbed, until—

Poor Little Mobi landed on the ground at the base of the big oak tree.

All around, his bear cub friends giggled and grinned. Little Mobi felt the tears drip, drop, drip off his nose.

Culture landed beside him. "What a sad bear you are!" he squawked. "How hard it is to live with a missing paw! You're helpless and little and a very big burden. You'll never climb trees with your friends. Wouldn't life be easier for everyone if you just ran away?"

Little Mobi's eyes welled up with more tears, when suddenly ...

... his mother crashed through the brush.

"Zip it, Culture!" growled Mother Bear.

"Go away; let us be. Mobi's life may be hard, but my son's still my son. I love him even more than all the treetops filled with fun. You say if he leaves, then I will be free, but it's my son's life, not mine, that means most to me."

Just as Culture promised, the years got tough, but Little Mobi got tougher, and bit by bit, he grew.

At last, little Mobi wasn't little any longer. Because of his missing paw, Mobi resolved to work harder, run faster, and climb higher.

His struggles gave him a big heart for others.

He traveled far and wide across Freedom Island,
defending the helpless wherever he went.

Just as the leaves were turning reddish-orange, Mobi came to visit Mother Bear. Her brown fur had turned silver-gray, and her walk, once so quick, was now a lumber. But that made Mobi love her even more.

Preparing for winter, the other bears chomped and chewed,
filling their tummies with food. From her den, Mother Bear
watched as Mobi searched day and night to find her berries.

One morning, as Mobi gathered Mother Bear's breakfast, Culture landed beside him. "What a tired bear you are," he squawked.

"How hard you work to keep your old, weak mother full. She takes all your time—you can't chase adventure or climb trees with friends. Wouldn't life be easier if you left and lived for yourself?"

"Zip it, Culture!" growled Mobi Bear.

"My life may be hard, but I'm still my mother's son, and I love her even more than all the treetops filled with fun. You say if I leave, then my life will be free, but it's my mom's life, not mine, that means most to me."

TO YOUR FAMILY

INTRODUCTION

Storybooks are great, but the lessons don't always make their way into our hearts and minds. BRAVE Books has created The BRAVE Challenge section to help drive home key lessons and values from each book. Each game can take 10 to 20 minutes.

BRAVE CHALLENGE KEY

 Read aloud to the children

 One child modification

 For parents only

 Roll the die for Culture

THE BRAVE CHALLENGE

OBJECTIVE

 Children, welcome to Team BRAVE! Your mission for this BRAVE Challenge is to defend Wiggamore Woods and Mother Bear from Culture the Vulture! Your goal is to score more points than Culture. Your first objective is to create a scoreboard with Team BRAVE vs. Culture.

Culture	Team BRAVE
|||	ЖН ||

While the children are creating the scoreboard be thinking about what they win if they defeat Culture! Here are a few ideas:

- Night out with parents
- Movie night
- Play the children's favorite game
- Putt-Putt golf
- Baking (and eating!) treats
- Bike ride
- Whatever gets your kiddos excited!

HOW THE POINTS WORK

 Team BRAVE can earn points in two ways!

First, by doing well in the games according to the rules of each game. Second, by giving thoughtful answers to the questions I ask after each game in the Talk About It section.

How does Culture score points? I will roll the die for Culture before each activity and also before the Talk About It section of each game. The number rolled on the die is the amount of points Culture gets for that activity. For example, if I roll a three, Culture gets three points for that activity.

Don't let me forget to record Team BRAVE and Culture's score on the scoreboard! If Team BRAVE has more points than Culture after all three games than you have successfully defended Wiggamore Woods. The prize for winning will be _____. Let's begin!

 The BRAVE Challenge works best with two or more children, but it still works with one child. If there is one child and two parents, then choose one parent to be on the same team as the child and keep the games the same.

INTRODUCING…

ELIZABETH JOHNSTON

Elizabeth Johnston is a popular conservative influencer who has spent her career bringing awareness to issues close to her heart, including the importance of God and the family. She helped BRAVE Books write this story and the BRAVE Challenge. She will be popping in to give you ideas on how you can explain these concepts to your child.

ELIZABETH SUGGESTS

"All lives are valuable! These activities and discussion points aim to help your child understand that all lives are worth protecting and all lives have the privilege of living: from the unborn, to the disabled, to the elderly."

GAME #1 - DEAD OR ALIVE

MATERIALS NEEDED

Something soft to land on, such as a pillow, and a six-sided die.

 Roll #1 - Roll the die and record Culture's score (from 1 to 6)

OBJECTIVE

 For this game, each member of Team BRAVE should place both hands on his or her knees and stand on a rug, a pillow, or a couch cushion on the floor. Every time I say the name of something alive, jump in the air and then act like that thing. If I say the name of something not alive, drop down onto the pillow, and then act like that thing.

If every child does the correct action (jump or drop) then Team BRAVE gains one point, but if even one teammate does not do the correct action, you don't get the point. Here we go!

• A rock	*Drop!*
• A fish	*Jump!*
• A robot	*Drop!*
• A baby	*Jump!*
• A baby inside a mommy	*Jump!*
• A chocolate chip cookie	*Drop!*

TALK ABOUT IT

 Roll #2 - Roll the die and record Culture's score (from 1 to 6)

Ask the following questions and award points based on the thoughtfulness of the answers.

1. How can you tell a rock is NOT alive?

2. How can you tell a fish IS alive?

3. How can you tell a baby inside a mommy IS alive?

─── BRAVE TIP ───
Remember to reward points for effort as well as correctness.

4. Which is worth more: a fish or a chocolate chip cookie? Why?

5. Just because living things are more important, does that mean non-living things aren't important? What are some examples of non-living things that are very important? *(Examples can include: sunlight, air, and books.)*

6. Which is worth more: a human baby or a fish? Why?

ELIZABETH SUGGESTS

"While both a fish and a human baby are alive, a baby is more valuable than a fish because human babies are made in the image of God. Fish are fun, but you, like all humans, are special in God's eyes."

Genesis 1:27 (ESV) "So God created man in his own image, in the image of God he created him; male and female he created them."

GAME #2 - FAVORITE THINGS

MATERIALS NEEDED

A reusable shopping bag for each BRAVE member, a timer, and a six-sided die.

 Roll #3 - Roll the die and record Culture's score (from 1 to 6)

OBJECTIVE

 In this game, all members of Team BRAVE will find their favorite thing that can fit inside these bags. When I say go, you'll have 90 seconds to find it and return to your spot. Once you find your favorite thing, put it inside the bag and make sure no one else on Team BRAVE can see it. We'll guess what you've chosen when you get back! Ready, set, go!

(Start the 90 second timer and send the kids out to gather their favorite things.)

Good job, everyone! Now, your teammates will join together to guess the item in your bag. Don't give any hints! They will have three guesses to come up with an answer. If they guess your item correctly, you will receive six points. After everyone's item has been guessed, we will take the average number of points awarded as our final score to add to the scoreboard. Remember, you cannot touch the bag when guessing.

(Choose a child to begin, and award points as directed.)

TALK ABOUT IT

 Roll #4 - Roll the die and record Culture's score (from 1 to 6)

Ask the following questions and award points based on the thoughtfulness of the answers.

1. What did you like most about the item you chose?

 Okay now that the game is over, put your items back in the bags. We don't need these any longer, so we'll just throw them away.

(Grab all the bags and begin walking towards the trashcan. Try to convince your kids that you actually mean to get rid of the items, but don't actually hurt them. When your kids begin to protest, stop.)

I'm kidding, I'm kidding! Everyone, calm down. Let's talk about this.

2. Why did you not want me to throw away your things?

3. How did it make you feel when I said I was going to throw your favorite thing away? Why?

4. When God made the world, he only made one thing that was like himself—people! We are his favorite creation. How do you think God feels when we hurt his favorite creation?

ELIZABETH SUGGESTS

"Help your children understand that when you spend time creating something, it hurts when others come and destroy it. God has created everything with a purpose and meaning. Because God finds joy in His creation, we must strive to protect it."

GAME #3 - GATHERING BERRIES

MATERIALS NEEDED

Six balls, a basket, a timer, and a six-sided die.

 Roll #5 - Roll the die and record Culture's score (from 1 to 6)

OBJECTIVE

 Each member of Team BRAVE will take turns gathering "berries" for Mother Bear. I'll blindfold the first team member and place six balls around the room. Your objective is to help the blindfolded team member move as many balls as possible into the basket in the center of the room within 120 seconds. To make it even harder, the berrypicking teammate can only use his left (or non-dominant) hand. He must put his right hand in a pocket and leave it there.

After the first teammate is finished, we'll record how many berries he gathered, reset the berries, and move to the next person. Each berry is worth a point for that person, and at the end, we'll average all the children's scores.

Ready, set, go!

TALK ABOUT IT

 Roll #6 - Roll the die and record Culture's score (from 1 to 6)

Ask the following questions and award points based on the thoughtfulness of the answers.

1. How did it feel not being able to see where the balls are and not being able to use both hands? Do you think you could have done it by yourself?

2. How do you think Mother Bear helped Mobi when he was a little baby? How hard would it have been for Little Mobi without Mother Bear?

3. Did Mother Bear love Little Mobi even when he was a baby and hard to care for? When did Mother Bear start loving Little Mobi?

4. When did God start loving you? Has he always loved you, even before you were inside your mom?

ELIZABETH SUGGESTS

"God has always loved you, even before you were born."

Jeremiah 1:5 (ESV) "Before I formed you in the womb I knew you."

5. God loves the vulnerable and weak in our world. How can we make God happy by showing love to the vulnerable and weak?

6. The villain in this book is named "Culture." What do you think this means?

ELIZABETH SUGGESTS

"Some elements of culture you may want to help your children recognize are: popular movies and music, words that people use, images and phrases trending on social media platforms, etc."

7. In the book, Culture the Vulture told Mobi and his mother to stay away from hard work. What do you think the culture around you is saying about hard work? Is that a good message to listen to?

TALLY ALL THE POINTS TO SEE WHO WON!

Submit comments to: Feedback@BRAVE.us

Make sure to check out our previous book in this saga!

Kevin the Elephant has always loved to sing. When a vulture named Culture suggests that Kevin is actually a bird, he embarks on an adventure exploring reality, identity, and truth. Kids will love following Kevin's exploits and participating in The BRAVE Challenge, a collection of games and discussion questions to help children think through the topic of gender identity.

Upcoming topics in this saga include: capitalism, cancel culture, Critical Race Theory, and the right to bear arms.

Visit www.BRAVEbooks.us to learn more today!